This book belongs to:

LogAN Scott Heyting

Quiet Bunny

To Nancy and Julie

Thanks to Nancy Kriebel, for inspiring me with your insight as a speech language pathologist to create an interactive story that targets sounds that are instrumental for early speech development and pre-reading/reading skills.

Library of Congress Cataloging-in-Publication Data Available

2 4 6 8 10 9 7 5 3 1

Published by Sterling Publishing Co., Inc.
387 Park Avenue South, New York, NY 10016

Distributed in Canada by Sterling Publishing
c/o Canadian Manda Group, 165 Dufferin Street
Toronto, Ontario, Canada M6K 3H6
Distributed in the United Kingdom by GMC Distribution Services
Castle Place, 166 High Street, Lewes, East Sussex, England BN7 1XU
Distributed in Australia by Capricorn Link (Australia) Pty. Ltd.
P.O. Box 704, Windsor, NSW 2756, Australia

Printed in China

Sterling ISBN 978-1-4027-5719-8

For information about custom editions, special sales, premium and
corporate purchases, please contact Sterling Special Sales
Department at 800-805-5489 or specialsales@sterlingpublishing.com.

Quiet Bunny

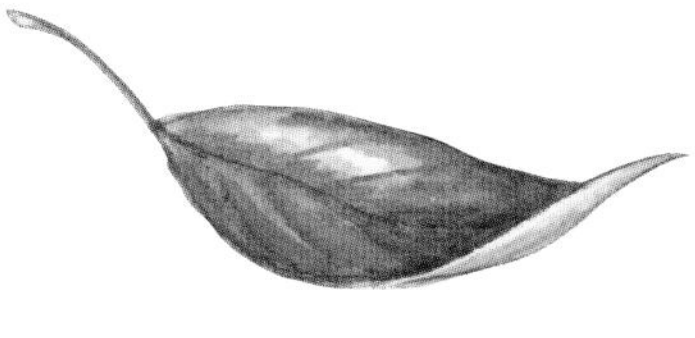

Lisa McCue

STERLING
New York / London

tWeet-tWeet-tWeet-tWeet

Quiet Bunny loves the sounds of the forest.

He loves the morning sounds of happy birds singing. . . .

SHHHHHhhhhhhhhhhhhhh

He loves the afternoon sound of the breeze rustling the leaves.

SHHhhhhhhhhhhhhhhh

But in the evening the sun sinks low and shadows from the trees grow long, and all of the bunnies hop to the meadow to listen to the night song.

This is the time Quiet Bunny loves most.

Tonight Quiet Bunny did not sit up tall and still like the other bunnies. Instead, he lay back in the soft grass, closed his eyes, and spread his ears wide to listen as the animals started to sing.

nnNNNnnnnNNNnnnn
ch-CHEET
ch-CHEET
ch-CHEET

First the cricket, *ch-cheet ch-cheet ch-cheet.*

Then the owl, *hoooooooooooot, hoooooooooooot.*

The snake, sssssssssssssss.

And the tiny mosquitoes, *nNNnnnnnnnNnnn.*

He could hear the bullfrogs by the pond, *croak, croak, croak.*

And the wolf howling at the moon, *ouuuuuuuuu.*

Quiet Bunny longed to join in, but whenever he opened his mouth, no sound came out.

When the first star twinkled in the night sky, Quiet Bunny thought, *Tonight I will make a wish. I wish for a sound so that I can sing in the night song.*

The next morning, Quiet Bunny woke up early to the birds singing,

Excited, he opened his mouth to join in, but he was as quiet as ever. *If only my wish had come true,* he thought, as he set off hopping through the forest.

At the edge of the pond Quiet Bunny watched an enormous bull frog puff up his throat. Quiet Bunny tried to do the same. The bull frog bellowed,

CROaK
CrOAK
CRoAK
CROaK

Quiet Bunny was silent.

Across the pond wading in the rushes, was a tall loon with his head thrown back as he sang,

Quiet Bunny threw his head back too, opened his mouth and sang . . . nothing.

Down the path Quiet Bunny saw a snake curled up on a rock basking in the sun. The snake lifted her head and with a forked tongue she hissed,

Quiet Bunny could lift his head as high as the snake, but his little pink bunny tongue made no sound.

All day long Quiet Bunny hopped
around the forest trying to hum
like the hummingbirds,

HmmMmmmMm

growl like the bear cub,

Grrrrrrrrrrrrr

and buzz like the bees.

As the day faded to dusk, a sad Quiet Bunny turned to head for the meadow.

Zoom! Overhead flew a bat,

wHa WhA whA
WhA wHa WhA Wha whA
whA wHa wHa

Startled, Quiet Bunny looked up. The sound was coming from the little bat's quick wings.

Quiet Bunny flapped his paws. No sound.

He flapped his ears. No sound.

He flapped his paws and his ears, but there was no *wha wha wha* from this soft fuzzy bunny.

Quiet Bunny noticed a cricket sitting on a long blade of grass, happily rubbing his hind legs together,

ch-CHeET ch-CHEET ch-CHEET

Quiet Bunny was sure he could do this. He held up his big furry feet and started to rub them together. He rubbed and rubbed and rubbed and rubbed.

HOOOOOOOT

Quiet Bunny stopped rubbing. Above him sat a large owl.

"I've been watching you, Quiet Bunny," said the owl. "It doesn't matter how hard you rub your feet together, or flap your ears, or puff up your cheeks, you will never make the sound of a cricket, or a bat, or a frog. You are a Quiet Bunny. Be whoooooo you are, and you will find your own bunny sound."

Who am I? Quiet Bunny wondered.

The wind whispered, SHHhhhhhhhhhhhhhhhhhhhhhh

Quiet Bunny wiggled his ears. "I am a bunny with large floppy ears who loves to listen to the forest sounds." Quiet Bunny blinked. "I am a bunny with curious eyes who loves to watch the sunset."

SHhhhhhhhhhhhhhhhhhhhhhhh

Quiet Bunny twitched his nose. "I am a bunny who loves to sniff the sweet scent of honeysuckle."

Quiet Bunny wiggled his toes. "I am a bunny with big furry feet who loves to hop, and right now I must hop to the meadow or I will miss the start of the night song."

But right in Quiet Bunny's way was a big hollow log.
With a running start, Quiet Bunny leaped onto the log landing with a . . .

THUMP!

tHUmP-da-DUM, tHuMp

Had Quiet Bunny made a sound? He tapped his foot on the log again, tap, tap, tap, and again a loud *THUMP, THUMP, THUMP* came out. He had made a sound!

Quiet Bunny leaped with joy, and started to dance. *Thump, thump, thump,* he started to tap a beat. *Thump-da-dum, thump-thump-da–dum, thump-thump–da-dum, thump-thump.*

tHUmP–da–DUM, tHuMp–tHUMp–da–dum

OUuUUUUUuuUuuuu
HOOOOOOT
tWeet
tWeet
Zzzzzz
SssSssSSsss
CROAK
CROAK
CROAK

Soon Quiet Bunny was surrounded by the other animals coming to see who had started the night song with such a wonderful beat. One by one they started to join in. And a sweet melody filled the meadow.

Lululuululu Lululuululu
wHa wHa
BzZzzzz
Grrrrrrrrrrrrr
HmmMmmm
ch-CHEET
ch-CHEET
HUmP-da-DUM, tHuMp-tHUMp-da-dum

Next time you go outside on a warm summer night, listen closely.

You just might hear Quiet Bunny leading the night song.